"I'VE KNOWN KISSES AFORE. NEVER HAVE I THOUGHT TO TASTE SO DEEPLY."

A quiver raced down Elienor's spine. "Unhand me!" she cried.

Alarik shook his head slowly, his lips brushing hers as he spoke. "Elienor, you cannot think to entice me," he whispered, "only to deny me after." At once, he claimed her lips—coaxing, tormenting, burning. Liquid fire flowed through her, and she feared she craved him with a madness that was shameful . . .

VIKING'S PRIZE

"A tantalizing tale of love and betrayal . . .
A sensual love story that will hold you in thrall!"
Lizabelle Cox, *Romantic Times*

"An absolutely endearing love story . . .
Tanya Anne Crosby at her best!"
Chronicle

D1006968

m,

Coeur